Dear Parents,

A love of reading is something we  book series is designed to encourage reading at points appropriate to most any reader. Our well-defined levels help you choose books that are best suited to your child's interests and ability. These colorful books tap into a child's imagination and build confidence for a lifelong love of reading.

Our Read Smart bookmarks reinforce your child's reading vocabulary through games and activities. Take the time to make reading more fun by following the simple instructions on the bookmark.

Reading is a voyage that can take your child into wonderful, enchanting places. We are delighted to join you on this journey.

 BEGINNING READER

For children who are ready to read their first books, know their letter sounds, and have developed an understanding of early phonics skills. Words include short vowels, simple plurals, and sight words.

 DEVELOPING READER

For children who are ready for longer sentences and more lines of print per page. Stories are richer and include a growing vocabulary. Words feature beginning consonant blends.

 CONFIDENT READER

For children who are ready for books with longer sentences and richer plots. Words are longer and feature ending consonant blends and simple suffixes.

 ADVANCED READER

For children who are ready for books with more complex plots, varied sentence structure, and full paragraphs. Words feature long vowels and vowel combinations.

ISBN 1-60143-481-2

Get That Ball

Written by **Paige Russell**
Illustrated by **Andy Norman & Patrick Kouse**

"I am at the beach," says Denzel. "I will have fun in the sun.

"I will hop, skip, and run.

"I will swim and play and—"

THUD!

"Oh no," says Denzel. "I did not see that rock.

"Now where is my ball?

I will go look for it."

"I like this spot," says Lou.

"Let me set down my pack.

"I can sit in the sun and have a snack.

"I will sip from my cup and—"

BAM!

"What was that?" asks Lou.
"Was it an egg? Did a big rock
hit me?"

"I cannot say," says Denzel.

"But did you see a ball?"

"That way," says Lou.

"Thanks," says Denzel. "I will go and get it."

"This is fun," says Zweeble.

"I like to play in the sand.

"I can pick up rocks and clams and crabs.

"See how I can stack up shells?

I have 1, 2, 3—"

SMACK!

"What was that? Was I hit by a bus? Did a big duck come and peck on my neck?"

"I cannot say," says Denzel.

"But did you see a ball?"

"That way," says Zweeble.

"Thanks!" says Denzel. "I will go and get it."

"Look at me," says Ella.

"This will be a big castle.

But I still have a lot to do."

PLOP!

"I am so sorry," says Denzel. "I saw that my ball hit you and—"

"I like it!" says Ella. "Thank you. Thank you, Denzel."

"That's OK," says Denzel. "It was my plan all along."